Dear Parent:
Your child's love of reading starts here!

Every child learns to read in a different way and at his or her own speed. Some go back and forth between reading levels and read favorite books again and again. Others read through each level in order. You can help your young reader improve and become more confident by encouraging his or her own interests and abilities. From books your child reads with you to the first books he or she reads alone, there are I Can Read Books for every stage of reading:

SHARED READING
Basic language, word repetition, and whimsical illustrations, ideal for sharing with your emergent reader

BEGINNING READING
Short sentences, familiar words, and simple concepts for children eager to read on their own

READING WITH HELP
Engaging stories, longer sentences, and language play for developing readers

READING ALONE
Complex plots, challenging vocabulary, and high-interest topics for the independent reader

ADVANCED READING
Short paragraphs, chapters, and exciting themes for the perfect bridge to chapter books

I Can Read Books have introduced children to the joy of reading since 1957. Featuring award-winning authors and illustrators and a fabulous cast of beloved characters, I Can Read Books set the standard for beginning readers.

A lifetime of discovery begins with the magical words "I Can Read!"

Visit www.icanread.com for information
on enriching your child's reading experience.

Flat Stanley at Bat. Text copyright © 2012 by the Trust u/w/o Richard C. Brown a/k/a Jeff Brown f/b/o Duncan Brown. Illustrations by Macky Pamintuan, copyright © 2012 by HarperCollins Publishers. All rights reserved. Printed in the United States of America. No part of this book may be used or reproduced in any manner whatsoever without written permission except in the case of brief quotations embodied in critical articles and reviews. For information address HarperCollins Children's Books, a division of HarperCollins Publishers, 195 Broadway, New York, NY 10007.
www.icanread.com

Library of Congress catalog card number: 2011926076
ISBN 978-0-06-143010-7 (trade bdg.)—ISBN 978-0-06-143012-1 (pbk.)

14 15 16 17 18   LP/WOR   10 9 8 7 6 5 4   ❖   First Edition

FLAT STANLEY
at Bat

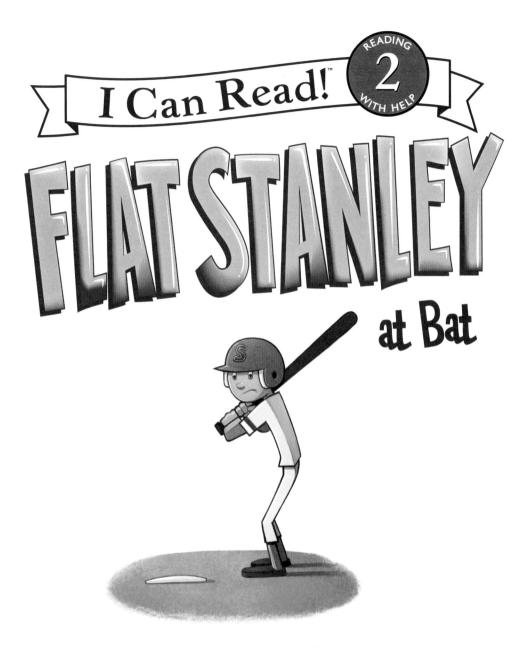

created by Jeff Brown
by Lori Haskins Houran
pictures by Macky Pamintuan

HARPER
An Imprint of HarperCollinsPublishers

Stanley Lambchop lived

with his mother,

his father,

and his little brother, Arthur.

Stanley was four feet tall,

about a foot wide,

and half an inch thick.

He had been flat ever since

a bulletin board fell on him.

Sometimes being flat

was a bit tricky.

When he turned sideways,

Stanley was hard to spot.

And a good gust of wind

could sweep Stanley off his feet.

But he never let his flatness

get in his way.

"I'm trying out for baseball,"
Stanley told Arthur one day.
Arthur helped Stanley practice.
Stanley hit a thousand pitches.
He caught a thousand fly balls.

Stanley's hard work showed

at tryouts.

"Congratulations," said Coach Bart.

"You're our new center fielder!"

Opening day was bright and breezy.

The teams ran onto the field.

"There's Stanley!" cried Arthur.

Mr. Lambchop snapped a picture.

Mrs. Lambchop cheered.

"Hooray for the other players, too,"

she added politely.

Stanley was the first batter.

He stepped up to home plate,

turned sideways,

and pulled back his bat.

The pitcher squinted at Stanley.

"This guy is so skinny," he said,

"I can hardly see where to throw."

He threw a pitch.

"Ball one," said the umpire.

Another pitch.

"Ball two," said the umpire.

Two more balls,

and Stanley earned a walk.

"Good job!" called Coach Bart.

Stanley's team played well.

By the ninth inning they led,

six to five.

The other team had one last chance.

Their best hitter came to bat

and blasted the ball toward the fence!

Just then, the breeze picked up.

Stanley ran and leaped into the wind.

WHOOSH! Up floated Stanley.

PLUNK went the ball into his glove!

"Great play!" Arthur called.

Not everyone agreed.

"No fair,"

yelled someone in the crowd.

"Are flat players even allowed?"

Stanley felt crushed.

That night, Stanley talked to Arthur.

"I'm a good player," he said.

"And not just because I'm flat.

But how can I prove it?"

"I think I know a way," Arthur said.

The day of the second game

was bright and breezy again.

But something was different.

"Stanley!" gasped Mrs. Lambchop.

Her son was not flat.

He was bursting out of his uniform!

Mrs. Lambchop gasped again.

"My nice clean laundry!"

A sock stuck out of Stanley's collar.

A purple frilly blouse

trailed from his pant leg.

"That's my favorite one!"

Mrs. Lambchop said.

There was no time to worry

about the clothes.

A batter smacked the ball
over Stanley's head!
Stanley ran and leaped into the wind.

But this time Stanley didn't float up,
and the ball didn't land in his glove.
It sailed right over the fence.

Soon it was Stanley's turn to bat.

The pitcher had no trouble

seeing where to pitch now.

"Strike one," called the umpire.

"Strike two. Strike three!"

In the bleachers, Arthur gulped.
Had he made a terrible mistake
helping Stanley unflatten himself?

The last inning rolled around.

The game was tied.

Stanley came to bat again.

He heard Arthur's voice

in the crowd.

"Come on, Stanley!

You can do it!"

The pitcher threw the ball . . .

and Stanley SMASHED it!

The ball flew into the outfield.

BAP! It bounced off the wall.

The right fielder ran to pick it up.

Meanwhile, Stanley tore

around the bases.

First base. Second base. Third base.

Stanley was headed home!

But so was the ball!

"Stanley, SLIDE!" shouted Coach Bart.

Arthur's heart raced.

If Stanley were still flat,

he could slide easily

under the catcher's glove.

But now?

Stanley stretched out his arms
and dove onto home plate.

There was a swirl of dirt and socks.

Then the umpire spread his arms.

"Safe!" he called.

"Wahoo!" Arthur hollered.

Mr. and Mrs. Lambchop clapped

so hard their hands hurt.

"No fair,"

yelled someone in the crowd.

"Look at the muscles on that kid.

Are players that big even allowed?"

Stanley grinned.

"Not so many socks next time,"
Mr. Lambchop called down to Stanley.

Mrs. Lambchop looked at Arthur.

"And NO blouses!"